USBORNE HOTSHOTS

FACE
PAINTING

USBORNE HOTSHOTS

FACE
PAINTING

Consultants: Chris Caudron and
Caro Childs of Lococo

Edited by Cheryl Evans and Alastair Smith
Designed by Karen Tomlins and Ian McNee

Illustrated by Chris Chaisty
Photographs by Ray Moller

Series editor: Judy Tatchell
Series designer: Ruth Russell

To find face paint suppliers, look in your Yellow
Pages telephone directory under **Costume
shops**. Call and ask if they supply
water-based face paint.

CONTENTS

4 Ready to paint

6 Basic techniques

8 Cats

10 Circus clown

12 Pierrot clown

14 Vampire

16 Monster

18 Butterfly

20 Garlands

22 Skull

24 Sunset scene

26 Robot

28 Bat

30 Party pieces

32 Index

Ready to paint

To paint the exciting faces in this book you need water-based face paints. These cost a little more than other kinds, but give much better results. You can buy them from toy shops or theatrical suppliers (see page 2).

Sponges

You can use ordinary make-up sponges or buy special, thick ones from face paint suppliers. It is useful to have two or three sponges to use.

Paints

The paints come in single pots or a palette. They will not harm most skins, but check for skin allergies first. They wash off with soap and water.

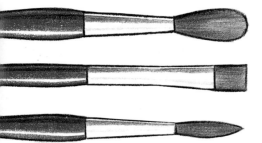

Paintbrushes

You need at least one fine brush and one thick one. They may have flat or pointed ends, which make different shapes when you paint with them.

Getting started

Wear old clothes, so it will not matter if you get paint on them (though it does wash off). Make sure your hands and the model's face are clean and dry. Tie back hair that falls over the model's face. Here you can see the best way to set yourself up to paint.

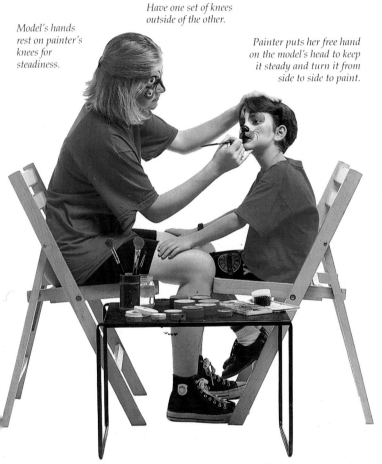

Have one set of knees outside of the other.

Model's hands rest on painter's knees for steadiness.

Painter puts her free hand on the model's head to keep it steady and turn it from side to side to paint.

Sit very close to your model, on chairs facing each other.

Place your paints and water on a table near your painting hand.

5

Basic techniques

Successful face painting relies on good brush control and on being able to put down areas of paint accurately. Here are the basic techniques.

Brush control

Hold the brush like a pencil, a little above the bristles, as shown on the left.

Get the bristles really wet, then wipe and roll them gently across the paint.

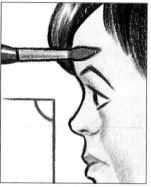

Paint with the brush at a right angle to the face. The red lines show this angle.

Lay the bristles flat on the face and press as you paint to make a thick line.

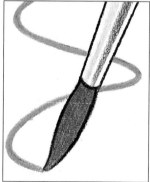

Lift the brush and paint with the tip to make a fine line or come to a point.

Sponging a base

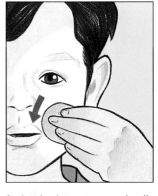

1. It is vital to learn how to sponge an even base. Wet a sponge and squeeze hard until no more drops come out. Rub the sponge lightly in circles over the paint.

2. Apply the paint evenly all over the face. Dab and push the sponge onto the face with a twist of the wrist. Don't try to sponge in long, dragging strokes.

3. Do the eyelids. Then ask the model to look up and work carefully under the eyes. Dab paint well into the creases around the nose, mouth and eye corners.

4. Check that the base is neat and even all over the face. Turn the model's face gently to each side to check that the paint on the chin line is not ragged.

7

Cats

You can do lots of versions of this cat face. Look at real cats' markings to do pet cats, or look at pictures of the big, wild cats. You can use your own imagination to create bright fantasy cats.

Always sponge the middle of the cat's face a paler shade than the outside. This makes the face seem to come forward, like an animal's muzzle.

Eyebrow whiskers

Paint a thick line along the brow bone, where the eyebrows are.

Lift the brush up and off at the end to make a point.

Repeat a few times. Lift the brush sooner each time.

Add extra dots and streaks, if you like.

The white lines suggest a cat's whiskery face.

The red strip under the nose looks like a split lip.

Paint the hands to match the face, for extra effect.

Painting some parts of the face a darker shade makes these parts sink into the face.

1. Sponge a base with a paler middle. Use a contrasting, darker paint to sponge shadows on the forehead and cheeks.

2. Fill a thick brush with white paint. Paint whiskery face markings out along the eyebrows. See how to do this on the opposite page.

3. Paint down the smile lines from nose to lips. Curve up and out to a point on the cheeks. Do this a few times, curving sooner each time.

4. Fill in above the top lip with white, except for a strip under the nose. Underline the eyes and outline the whiskers in red.

5. Paint the end of the nose, the strip you left below it, under the tip of the nose, and the top lip in the contrasting red paint.

6. Scatter several whisker dots all over the white patches above the top lip. Finally, paint the bottom lip with shiny metallic gold paint.

9

Circus clown

Traditionally, every clown invents his own style of face paint to please himself, so no two clowns ever look the same.

The pictures on the right show you the basic way to paint a clown's face. Look at the big photograph on the opposite page and the pictures below for more ideas.

Mouths

Paint a big mouth over and outside of the lips. The simplest sort of mouth to do is a blobby, sausage shape.

Curved down looks sad.

Curved up looks happy.

Eyebrows

Curved brows

Shaggy brows

Paint eyebrows above the real ones. Happy clowns can have bright eyebrows. Black eyebrows look more scary.

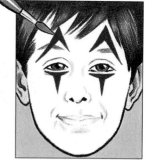

1. Sponge a white base. Paint thick eyebrows any shape you like. Underline the eyes and do a thin triangle down from the middle of each line. Ask your model to look up as you paint under the eyes.

2. Paint a red nose and a big red mouth. This clown's mouth extends right out onto the cheeks and ends in big red dots. If you like, you can add more bright shapes to the face.

10

This clown has thick, pointed eyebrows.

The eyelids have been painted up to the eyebrows, and decorated with spots.

Stars or spots are good decorations.

Leave a streak of white in the cheek dots to make them look shiny.

Pierrot clown

Pierrot (say pee-air-oh) clowns are beautiful, but often sad. Take time to do a thorough, even, white base first. Then the few strong details show up well.

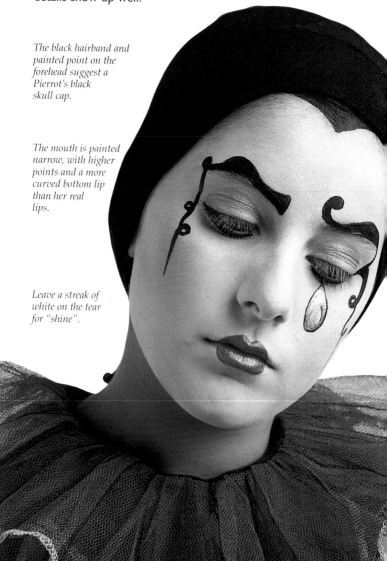

The black hairband and painted point on the forehead suggest a Pierrot's black skull cap.

The mouth is painted narrow, with higher points and a more curved bottom lip than her real lips.

Leave a streak of white on the tear for "shine".

1. Carefully sponge a white base. Then sponge the cheeks lightly with pale mauve or blue.

2. Load a brush with black paint to do fancy eyebrows. Curl them down onto the cheeks.

3. Paint a fine black line under each eye. Outline a big teardrop shape under one eye only.

4. Paint the eyelids delicately up to the line of the eye socket. Do a gold tear and pink lips.

Tip

This face works best if the two sides are not quite the same: paint different eyebrow shapes in step 2.

Vampire

A supernatural face, such as this, needs a spooky, unearthly-looking base. Work on a subtle base first, then add the details.

1. Sponge a white base. Shade it in grey (see below). With black on a brush, paint wicked, shaggy eyebrows and underline the eyes.

2. Outline the lips in black and paint fangs down from the corners of the top lip. When they dry, touch up the fangs with more white.

3. When the fangs are dry again, add a discreet droplet of scarlet blood on their tips. Fill the lips in with deep red paint.

Changing shape

You can make any face look thinner by clever shading. Start with a creepy base such as white, green or mauve. Shading should be darker so sponge on top of the base, as described below, with a little black, dark mauve or deep purple.

Shade the eye sockets. This makes the eyes seem to sink deeper.

Make the cheeks look hollow by darkening under the cheek bones.

Stroke the sponge down both sides of the nose so it looks lean and bony.

Shade along both of the outside edges of the chin.

14

You can sponge black onto fair hair. It will wash out.

Shade in sideburns with black paint, if you like.

Shaded nose looks thin and bony.

Paint the lip outline just outside of the real lips.

Monster

Purple, yellow, green and dark blue are all good for monster faces. Here, you can see how to do scales to make them even more frightening.

The black ovals make the eyes stand out and look startling.

The scales on the face make the monster look like a reptile.

The gold forked tongue adds a mythical touch.

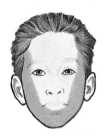

1. For a reptile, sponge yellow from forehead to mouth in a rough "U". Sponge the rest of the face green, blending where they meet.

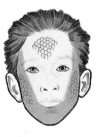

2. With dark green or black on a thin brush, paint scales using overlapping curved shapes in a triangle up the forehead and cheeks.

3. Do black ovals around the eyes and over the eyebrows, and triangles on the sides of the nose. Paint an oblong around the top lip.

4. Paint white fangs down from the corners of the lips. With gold paint, put a forked tongue over the lower lip and onto the chin.

5. When it is dry, fill the rest of the lower lip with black. Add a dash of dark green or gold inside each of the scales, if you like.

Butterfly

How you place a butterfly on a face is important. The shape must be the same on both sides. Paint the outlines carefully, then you can fill them in as brightly as you like. The left side is usually harder for right-handed people to draw. The right side is harder if you are left-handed. Do the side you find harder first. It is easier to make the second side match.

This butterfly is based on a rainbow. You could try your own pattern.

Correcting mistakes

If the sides don't match, change both until they do, as shown in red. You can only do it by making them bigger.

To make the wings match you must add the "wrong" lines to each. They will blend in when you paint over them.

18

1. With a fine brush, sweep a line up the forehead from the top of the nose. Curve it down beside and then under the eye, back to where you started.

2. Starting in the same place by the nose, paint another line that curves around the cheek, about down to the level of the bottom of the ear.

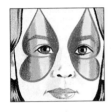

3. Do the other side of the face to match (see opposite page if you make a mistake). Fill the shapes in brightly. Paint from the nose out to the edges.

4. With a thin brush and white paint, make a long, smooth loop around each eyebrow. Do another loop in the middle of each bottom wing.

5. With white, make small loops around the big ones. Try not to lift your brush off the face. Then do a scalloped edge all around the wings.

6. Streak a long, red body down the nose (it must join the wings at the top). Add a round head, feelers and contrasting stripes on the body.

Garlands

A garland looks nice draped across the forehead and down beside the eyes, curling onto the cheeks. The steps below show you how to paint a garland. At the bottom you can see how to do some different kinds of flowers.

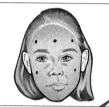

1. Sponge a two-tone blue base. Add some pink to the forehead, cheeks and chin. Place dots where you want to put the middles of your biggest flowers.

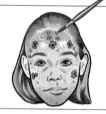

2. Add the big flowers' petals. Now scatter small dots in between them, where you will put smaller flowers. Then add these flowers' petals, too.

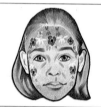

3. It is best to end with a small flower on each cheek. Leaves can link flowers and fill in any gaps. Join them with thin, green stems, if you like.

Rose	*Violet*	*Primrose*
With a thin brush, paint a pink spiral. Lay the brush down and move it around the edge to make three open petals.	Do a yellow dot. Lay down a brush lightly for petals. Do two above and three below. Press harder for bigger petals.	Do a small orange cross. For yellow petals, press a brush down, lift it up, then press again, to one side and overlapping.

The two sides of the garland do not need to match exactly.

For a finishing touch you could wear glossy lipstick.

Anemone

Do a large black dot. Put red on a thick brush, lay it down beside the dot and move it around a little to make a blob.

Daisy

Do a yellow dot. Load a pointed brush with white. For a petal, lay it down pointing at the dot, then lift it.

Leaves

Do leaves in pairs, with one at the end, by laying down the brush. Their shape depends on the brush (see page 4).

21

Skull

This is a face to frighten your friends or wear to a scary Halloween party. There are some more party ideas on pages 30-31. To start the face, sponge a white base. With a very dry sponge, dab just a little green around the edges.

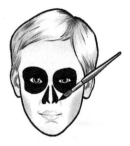

1. On top of the white base, sponge grey shadows under the cheekbones. Paint a black circle around each eye. Ask your model to close his eyes while you paint his eyelids.

2. Paint two long, black triangles on the end of the nose to look like the holes where the skull's nose used to be. The triangles end in curves around the tops of the nostrils.

3. Outline a big, black oblong around the mouth. Paint black lines across it, leaving white, lumpy "tooth" shapes. When the black is dry, touch up the teeth with more white paint.

4. Paint jagged, forked cracks in black across the skull. Paint white lines beside them to make the cracks look as if they are really deep. Use a fine brush for these thin cracks.

*Cover hair with
black material or
a hood to get the
total spooky
effect.*

Sunset scene

The secret of this face is to blend paint in several bands across the face. Then add a few simple shapes to suggest your scene. Silhouettes can be very effective. These are outline shapes completely filled in so you recognize what they are by their shape, not by details on them. You can see some silhouettes on the face shown here.

1. Sponge the whole lower part of the face turquoise from the chin up to about level with the bottom of the ears.

Dab to blend the strata together.

Don't overcrowd the face with details.

Branches curve with the shape of the face.

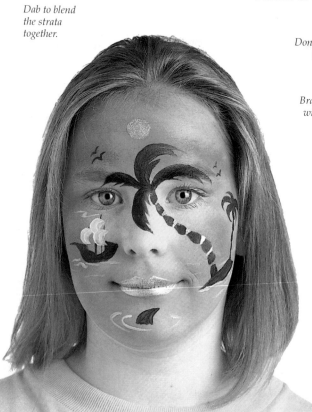

2. Working quickly, while the turquoise is still damp, blend yellow up over the nose and cheeks and across the eyelids.

3. Sponge pink over the eyebrows and purple on the forehead. Give the face some shape with purple shading.

4. Load a medium brush with black and paint four palm branches. See the box below for how to do them.

5. Do a line of black blobs with spaces between them for the trunk. Each time, press the brush down, then lift it.

6. You can add more silhouettes if you want to, such as a shark's fin or a ship. V-shapes in the sky are birds.

7. Streak gold on the joints of the trunk as if it is caught by the setting sun. Make the face glow with a gold sun and gold lips.

Palm branches

Start with the tip of the brush, press and make a thick curve. Then lift off to make a point.

From the same spot, curve a branch over each brow, one down the nose and one up the forehead.

Add fine, spiky curves down from underneath each main curve to make palm fronds (leaves).

Robot

Silver and gold paint do not show up very well by
themselves on most skins. If you mix them with green,
blue or mauve, though, they make a shiny, metallic effect
which is great for robots, monsters or aliens.

*The dots look like
rivets, which are
used to hold
metal sheets
together.*

*You could paint gold
dots on the corners
of the eye patches, to
look like gold rivets.*

1. Mix deep blue with silver and sponge a base. With dark blue on its own, sponge straight-edged shadows from cheekbones to chin.

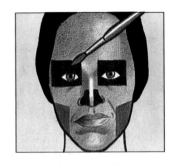

2. Using a brush, paint big, black squares around the eyes and fill them in. Paint thin black rectangles on the nose above the nostrils.

3. Paint a solid black oblong shape around the mouth. Do some thin, straight lines on the face, to look like metal sheets joined together.

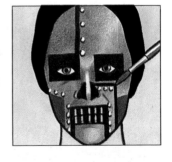

4. Place small white dots along the lines. Outline half of each dot in black. Add thin gold lines across the mouth, to make it look like a metal grille.

Bat

Wear black clothes to complete
the sinister effect of a bat design.
If you have light hair, wear
something dark on your head.

*Do gold details on
the black when
it is very dry.*

*Give the bat gold
eyes and streaks
across the body.*

*Paint
lips black
to complete
the face.*

Do the outline on the side you find hardest first.

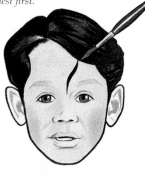

Do both wing outlines before filling in.

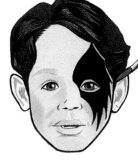

1. Sponge a yellow base. With black on a brush, slant a line up the forehead from the top of the nose to make a big point above the eye.

2. Do looping points down the side of the face and two long points down to about mouth level. Curve back up to the top of the nose.

Fill in from middle to edge of shapes.

Two or three gold lines fork from same place.

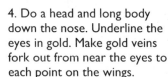

3. Do the other side to match. Outline a circle around the eye sockets and just under the eyes. Fill the rest of the wings in with black.

4. Do a head and long body down the nose. Underline the eyes in gold. Make gold veins fork out from near the eyes to each point on the wings.

Party pieces

You can use your face painting skills to have fun at parties. You could paint faces on a theme, or do a variety of your best faces on your friends. Here are some more ideas.

Lion

Do a cat face (see pages 8-9) with a yellow-brown base and white muzzle. Lions have a beard so sponge the chin white, too. Try to make the hair stick out like a lion's mane.

Valentine

Paint a special garland (see pages 20-21) for Valentine's Day. Do a white base and pink cheeks. Add hearts and ribbon. What would you paint for a Mothers' or Fathers' Day face?

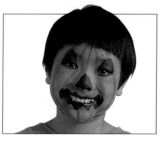

Pumpkin

Do an orange base. Paint red curved stripes down the face that meet at the chin. Do black triangles over the eyes and on the end of the nose, and a black zig-zag mouth to make a carved pumpkin.

Apple

Do a Halloween apple with a green base and pink cheeks. Put leaves and a stem on the forehead. Paint half a worm on the cheek, with a black circle around the end to look like a hole in the apple.

Christmas tree

Sponge a white base. Paint a green fir tree down the nose. The branches spread out onto the cheeks. Do a brown trunk from between the nostrils to the top lip and add decorations as you like. Paint red lips.

Strongman

Do a white base and blush pink cheeks. Add thick, black curly eyebrows and a line under each eye. Paint a black, twirly moustache and red lips. This face could also belong to a circus ringmaster.

Sports mad

Sponge opposite quarters of the face white. Sponge the other quarters to match the gear of a sports' team that you support. When the white is dry, use a brush to add stripes to match the other quarters.

Japanese doll

On a white base, sponge a pink band from brows to nose tip. Do a white line down the nose. Outline the eyes using black, making a point at the side. Paint sloping black brows. Do a small, red mouth.

Index

apple 30

bat 28-29
brush control 6
brushes 4, 6
butterfly 18-19

cats 8-9, 30
  whiskers 8, 9
Christmas tree 31
circus clown 10-11
  eyebrows 10
  mouths 10
clowns
  circus 10-11
  Pierrot 12-13

eyebrows 10
  curved 10
  shaggy 10, 14
  thick, pointed 11
  whiskers 8, 9

face shape, changing
8, 9, 14
flowers
  anemone 21
  daisy 21
  primrose 20
  rose 20
  violet 20

garlands 20-21
  flowers 20, 21
  leaves 21

Halloween 22, 30

Japanese doll 31

leaves 21
lion 30

mistakes, correcting
18
monsters 16-17, 26
  robot 26-27
  scales 16, 17
mouths 10

paints, water-based 4
  suppliers 2
palm branches 25
party ideas 22, 30-31
  apple 30
  Christmas tree 31
  Halloween 22, 30
  Japanese doll 31
  lion 30
  pumpkin 30
  sports fan 31
  strongman 31
  Valentine 30

Pierrot clown 12-13
preparation 4-5
  brushes 4, 6
  paints 4
  sponges 4
  pumpkin 30

reptile 16, 17
  scales 16, 17
ringmaster 31
rivets 26
robot 26-27

scales 16, 17
shading 8, 9, 14, 15
silhouettes 24, 25
skin allergies 4
skull 22-23
sponges 4
sponging a base 7
sports fan 31
strongman 31
sunset scene 24-25

techniques, basic 6-7
  brush control 6
  sponging a base 7,
  8, 9

Valentine 30
vampire 14-15

This book is based on material previously published in *The Usborne Book of Face Painting*.

First published in 1995 by Usborne Publishing Ltd, Usborne House, 83-85 Saffron Hill, London EC1N 8RT, England.

Copyright © Usborne Publishing Ltd 1993, 1995

Printed in Italy. First published in America August 1995. AE